ALICE
IN WONDERLAND
The Mad Hatter's Tea Party

WRITTEN BY

Lewis Carroll

ILLUSTRATED BY

Eric Puybaret

ALICE
IN WONDERLAND
The Mad Hatter's Tea Party

A MODERN RETELLING BY

Joe Rhatigan &
Charles Nurnberg

MoonDance

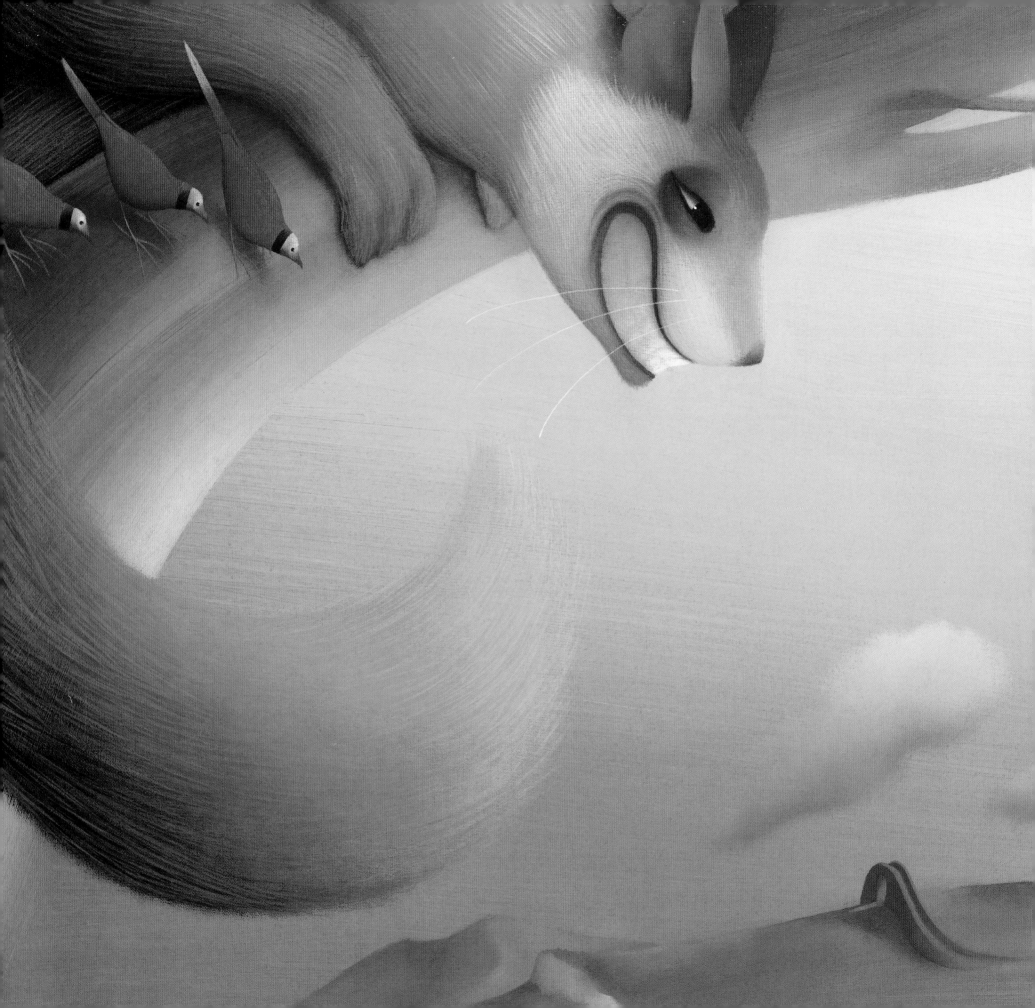

Small as a mouse and so very lost in Wonderland, Alice asked, "Which way do I go?"

"Well, that depends on where you want to go."

"Who said that?" asked Alice. She turned this way and that until she spotted the Cheshire Cat, who had long claws and a great many teeth. He was grinning at Alice.

"I don't know where I want to go," said Alice, "as long as I get somewhere."

"Then it doesn't matter. Why don't you go and visit the March Hare and the Mad Hatter?"

POOF—the Cat slowly disappeared, except for his big, toothy smile.

"Well! I've often seen a cat without a grin," thought Alice, "but a grin without a cat? It's the most curious thing I ever saw in all my life."

Alice walked to the March Hare's house, and there he
was with the Mad Hatter and the Dormouse, crowded
together at a large table set for a tea party.
"How lovely, a tea party! Can I sit?" asked Alice.
"No room! No room!" they cried.
"There's plenty of room,"
said Alice as she sat down—PLOP
—in a great big chair.

"Have some juice," said the March Hare.

"I don't see any," said Alice.

"That's because there isn't any," said the Hare.

The three strange creatures giggled.

The Mad Hatter saw that the Dormouse had fallen asleep. So he poured tea on his nose to wake him up.

Alice helped herself to tea and bread while the sleepy Dormouse told a story of three little sisters who lived in a well filled with candy—

YUM!

"The sisters couldn't have done that, you know," Alice said. "They would have gotten sick."

"Shhhhhhh," said the Mad Hatter. "If you can't be nice, you can finish the story yourself!"

Then the Mad Hatter shouted:

"I want a clean cup. Let's all move over!"

They all moved, which made a huge mess! Alice decided it was time to leave.

"HMMPH—This was the silliest tea party I ever was at in all my life!"

Alice walked into the woods and soon *found* a tree with a tiny door! ZIP—in she went and *found* a beautiful garden. She walked toward three gardeners who looked a lot like playing cards.

"Here comes the Queen!" yelled a gardener pointing down a path. A parade of soldiers, children, guests, and the White Rabbit stomped through the garden. Finally the King and Queen of Hearts arrived.

Everybody bowed to the King and Queen, but not Alice.
This made the Queen angry. She marched over to
Alice and yelled, "Off with her head!"

"Nonsense!" said Alice. "You shall do no such thing."

The very angry Queen stared at Alice. But after a
moment she said, "Well, okay. Can you play croquet?"

"Yes," Alice replied.

"Come on then." The Queen pulled Alice along
by the arm.

Alice had never seen such a curious croquet ground. The balls were hedgehogs, the mallets were live flamingos, and the playing-card soldiers had to double themselves up to make the arches.

While chasing her hedgehog ball, Alice saw a head pop up out of nowhere. The Cheshire Cat!

"How are you getting on?" he asked.

"There are no rules to this game and the Queen cheats!"

The Queen, bothered by the Cat, declared,
"Off with his head!" But nobody knew how to
remove a head without a body, and soon the Cat's
head just faded away.

Just then a soldier yelled, "The trial's beginning!"

"What trial?" asked Alice. But the whole court rushed—ZOOM—to the castle without telling her.

Everybody was there: the soldiers, the knave, the White Rabbit, and even Bill the Lizard.

The White Rabbit cried out "Silence in the court!" and then read the charges:

"THE QUEEN OF HEARTS,
SHE MADE SOME TARTS,
ALL ON A SUMMER DAY:
THE KNAVE OF HEARTS,
HE STOLE THOSE TARTS,
AND TOOK THEM
QUITE AWAY!"

The White Rabbit called the *first witness*: the Mad Hatter, who was so nervous he took a bite out of his teacup–CRUNCH! Then the next witness was called:

Alice!

Meanwhile, Alice was growing bigger and **bigger**, and she knocked over the witness stand. "Oh, I beg your pardon!"

"Hold your tongue!" yelled the Queen. "Who cares what you say?" said Alice, who had grown to her full size. "You're nothing but a pack of playing cards!"

"Off with her head!" screamed the Queen at the top of her voice. At this, all the soldiers rose up into the air and came *flying* down on poor Alice.

Suddenly, Alice found herself back on the bank of the river near her home.

"Wake up, Alice," said her big sister.

"Oh, I've had such a curious dream," said Alice.

Alice told her sister of her time in Wonderland.

"It was curious, but now it's time for tea. It's getting late," her sister said.

Alice got up and ran home, thinking what a wonderful dream it had been.

For Héloïse — E.P.

To my sons, Jeremy, Peter, and David, and the daughters I have been lucky enough to
gain through their marriages, Amy and Michelle — you all are special, and have made me
so very proud of the wonderful people you have become. And, as always and each day,
to my love, Barbara, for everything. — C.N.

For Ella & Clara — J.R.

Illustrator's Note

This second part of *Alice in Wonderland* is a fascinating entry into the imagination,
where wonder is mixed with anguish. The ambiguous characters nonetheless have a unique
personality, and the story as a whole is a magnificent source of inspiration for an illustrator.
Wonderland will be an incredible playground for artists for a long time!

About Lewis Carroll

Charles Lutwidge Dodgson (1832–1898), better known by his pen name, Lewis Carroll,
was born in Daresbury, Cheshire, England. The third of eleven children, Dodgson proved
himself an entertainer at a young age, performing plays and giving readings for his many siblings.
He was also known for his intellect, and went on to win many academic prizes in school,
especially for mathematics. A master of wordplay, logic puzzles, and later, photography,
Dodgson is best known for his two books following the incredible adventures of a young girl
named Alice. Begun as a way to entertain three little girls on a boating trip in 1862,
today *Alice's Adventures in Wonderland* (1865) and *Through the Looking Glass* (1871)
are among the most quoted works of literature in history, with unforgettable
characters permanently entrenched in our culture.